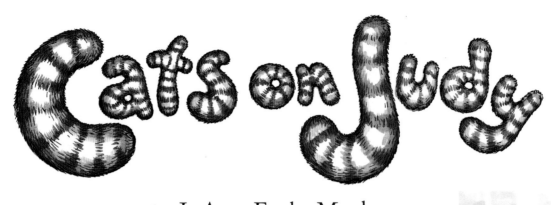

Cats on Judy

by JoAnn Early Macken

illustrated by Judith DuFour Love

WHISPERING COYOTE PRESS
Boston

For my family, especially Gene, Jimmy, Billy, and, of course, Judy
—J.E.M.

To my father, for his neverending faith in me
and his boundless love
—J.D.L.

Published by Whispering Coyote Press
480 Newbury Street, Suite 104, Danvers, MA 01923
Text copyright © 1997 by JoAnn Early Macken
Illustrations copyright © 1997 by Judith DuFour Love

10 9 8 7 6 5 4 3 2 1

Book design and production by *The Kids at Our House*
Text set in 20-point Garamond 3

Library of Congress Cataloging–in–Publication Data

Macken, JoAnn Early.
Cats on Judy / written by JoAnn Early Macken; illustrated by Judith DuFour Love.
p.   cm.
Summary: Judy's cats stay close by, keeping her company from morning through the night.
ISBN 1–879085–73–9
[1. Cats—Fiction.   2. Stories in rhyme.]
I. Love, Judith DuFour, ill.   II. Title.
PZ8.3.M187Cat   1997
[E]—dc20   96–44939
                                                                          CIP
                                                                          AC

Judy sleeps with cats on her bed,

One in her arms and one on her head.

With one on her head and one in her arms,

She can't resist their fuzzy charms.

She rather likes their company
Because they keep her warm, you see.
Because they keep her warm and snug
Just like a wiggly, squirmy hug.

So she's content to get her rest
With one on her knees and one on her chest.
With one on her chest and one on her knees
There's no chance she'll ever freeze.

Judy thinks they're very sweet,
One on her back and one on her feet.

With one on her feet and one on her back,
They snuggle in their cozy sack.

She cannot make them go away.
When she rolls over, so do they.

When they roll over, so does she.
Oh, cats are such good company!

And so they dream the whole night through.

When Judy wakes up, the cats do, too.

When the cats wake up, they all meow
So Judy knows it's time for chow.

And into the kitchen for breakfast she goes,
With one at her heels and one at her toes.

With one at her toes and one at her heels
She makes the most delightful meals.

And after each delicious treat
The hungry cats and Judy eat,
The cats curl up in Judy's lap
And settle down for a long cat nap.

And so she goes from day till night
With one on her left and one on her right,
One on her table and one on her chair
Judy's cats are everywhere!